Diary of a Wombat

written by
Jackie French

illustrated by
Bruce Whatley

HarperCollins *Children's Books*

First published in hardback in Australia by HarperCollins*Publishers* Pty Limited in 2002
First published in paperback in Great Britain by HarperCollins Children's Books in 2005

   9 10
978-0-00-721207-1

Visit our website at: www.harpercollins.co.uk

Bruce Whatley used acrylic paints to create the illustrations for this book.

Printed and bound in Great Britain by Martins the Printers

To Mothball, and all the others.
JF

Thanks for letting me play, Jackie.
This was fun.
BW

Monday

Morning: Slept.

Afternoon: Slept.

Evening: Ate grass.

Scratched.

Night: Ate grass.

Slept.

Tuesday

Morning: Slept.

Afternoon: Slept.

Evening: Ate grass.

Night: Ate grass. Decided grass is boring.

Scratched. Hard to reach the itchy bits.

Slept.

Wednesday

Morning: Slept.

Afternoon: Mild cloudy day.

Found the perfect dustbath.

Discovered flat, hairy creature
invading my territory.

Fought major battle with
flat, hairy creature.

Won the battle.

Demanded a carrot.

The carrot was delicious.

Evening: Demanded more carrots.

No response.

Chewed hole in door.

Ate carrots.

Scratched.

Went to sleep.

Bashed up rubbish bin
till carrots appeared.

Ate carrots.

Began new hole in soft dirt.

Went to sleep.

Friday

Morning: Slept.

Afternoon: Discovered new
scratching post.

Evening: Someone has filled in my new hole.

Soon dug it out again.

Night: Worked on hole.

Saturday

Morning: Moved into new hole.
Afternoon: Rained.

New hole filled up with water.
Moved back into old hole.

Evening: Discovered even more carrots.
Never knew there were so many carrots in the world.
Carrots delicious.

Night: Finished carrots.

Slept.

Sunday
Morning: Slept.
Afternoon: Slept.
Evening: Slept.

Night: Offered carrots at the back door.

Why would I want carrots when I feel like rolled oats?
Demanded rolled oats instead. Humans failed
to understand my simple request.
Am constantly amazed how dumb humans can be.

Chewed up one pair of boots, three cardboard boxes,
eleven flowerpots and a garden chair
till they got the message.

Ate rolled oats.

Scratched. Went to sleep.

Monday

Morning: Slept.

Afternoon: Felt energetic.
Wet things flapped against
my nose on my way to the back door.

Got rid of them.

Demanded oats AND carrots.
Only had to bash the rubbish bin
for five minutes before they arrived.

Evening: Have decided that humans
are easily trained and make quite good pets.

Night: Dug new hole
to be closer to them.

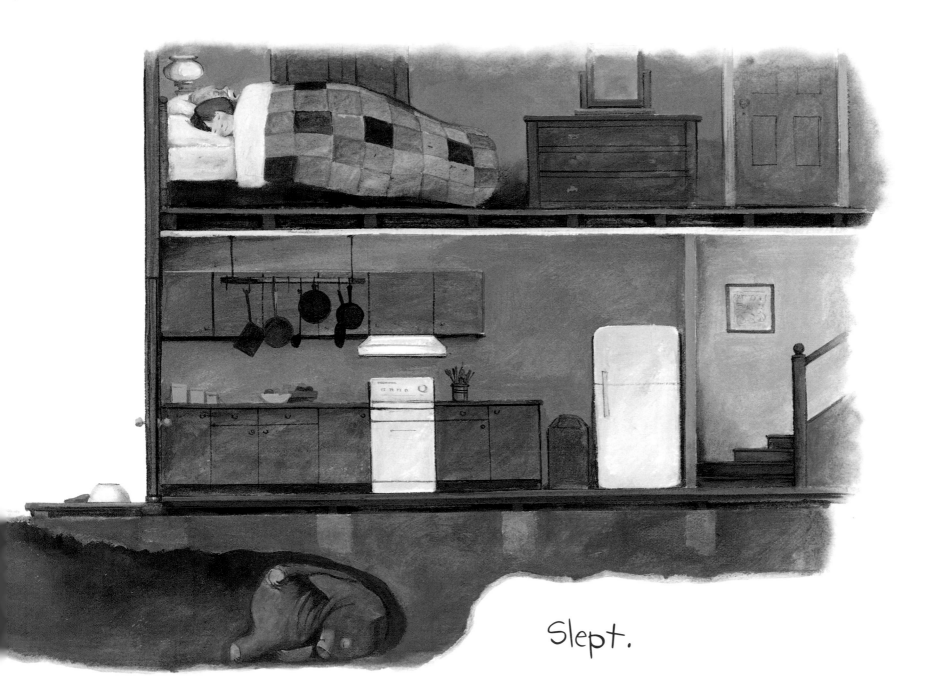

Slept.